Contents

JJ Rabbit and the Monster

One morning JJ Rabbit looked out
of his burrow. He saw some
footprints in the sand – great,
big, round footprints.
He called to Mole.

JJ Rabbit and the Monster

NICOLA MOON

Illustrated by
ANT PARKER

KING*f*ISHER

To Rosalind – N.M.
To Cathy Carrot – A.P.

KINGFISHER

An imprint of Kingfisher Publications Plc
New Penderel House, 283-288 High Holborn
London WC1V 7HZ

First published by Kingfisher 1999
4 6 8 10 9 7 5
4TR/0402/TWP/FR/GKBOMA115

A CIP catalogue record for this book
is available from the British Library.

ISBN 0 7534 0166 5

Printed in Singapore

"Did you see who made
these great, big, round footprints
outside my burrow last night?"
"No," said Mole.
"I was busy hunting
for worms."

5

JJ called to Owl.
"Did you see who made
these great, big, round
footprints outside
my burrow last night?"

"No," said Owl.
"I was flying over
the fields."

JJ called to Squirrel.

"Did *you* see who made these great, big, round footprints outside my burrow last night?"

"No," said Squirrel.

"I was away visiting my cousins."

"Was *nobody* here last night?" said JJ.

"Was I all alone?

All alone with a . . . with a . . .

MONSTER outside my burrow?"

He was beginning to feel a bit

frightened.

The animals all studied the footprints.

"They're big," said Mole.

"They're round," said Owl.

"They're strange," said Squirrel.

"They're scary," said JJ,

"and they're outside *my* burrow."

9

That night, JJ couldn't sleep.

He imagined all sorts of monsters
and giants clumping about,
making footprints in the sand
outside his burrow.

He tossed and he turned
until he was quite worn out.

Then he heard a strange noise.

Clump.

Clump.

Clump.

It grew louder and louder.

Clump.

Clump.

Clump!

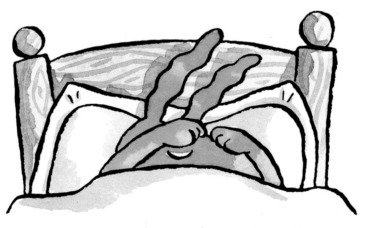

Now it was right outside his door.

Poor JJ was too frightened to look.

He lay shivering under his bedclothes.

He was still there in the morning
when Mole came to find him.
"It came again!" JJ told Mole.
"The *MONSTER* came again.
And I was all alone in my burrow.
Anything could have happened!"
JJ was trembling to the tips
of his whiskers.

Mole called Owl and Squirrel,

and they all studied the footprints again.

"They're very big," said Mole.

"They're very round," said Owl.

"They're very strange," said Squirrel.

"And very, very scary," said JJ.

The other animals agreed that the

footprints were very scary indeed.

That night, Mole, Owl and Squirrel
decided to stay with JJ
to try to see the Monster.
After supper, they all crowded
into his burrow.
Nobody was feeling very brave.
They waited.

14

Every time a twig snapped,

or a leaf rustled,

JJ dived under his bed.

They waited and waited

until Mole and Squirrel

were almost asleep.

Then they heard a strange noise.

15

Clump.

Clump.

Clump.

It came closer and closer.

Clump.

Clump.

Clump!

"It's coming to get me!"

squealed JJ.

"It's right outside,"

whispered Squirrel.

"Go and look,"

said Mole.

"No, *you* go and look,"

said Squirrel.

"We'll all go and look together,"
said Owl.
The animals crept towards the door.

Together they opened the door
a tiny crack,

just enough to peep out.

"What is it?" said Squirrel,

who didn't dare look.

"I don't know," said Mole,

her eyes tightly shut.

"It's a monster,

it's a monster!"

squealed JJ,

his paws

over his eyes.

Owl was the only one
brave enough to look.
He flung open the door . . .

"It's Badger!" he cried.

Sure enough, there was Badger.

He was carrying a huge bundle.

Clump.

Clump.

Clump!

went the bundle,

leaving big round marks in the sand.

The marks looked *exactly*

like footprints.

"What are you doing?" asked Squirrel.

"Moving house," puffed Badger.

"There's always such a lot . . .

of stuff to carry . . . when you

move house."

"JJ thought you were

a scary monster," said Owl.

"He was frightened,

so we stayed the night with him."

"*I* wasn't frightened," said Squirrel.

22

"Neither was I!" said Mole.

"It was only Badger, after all," said Owl.

"Yes," said JJ, looking at the marks the bundle had left in the sand, "but it *might* have been a monster."

JJ Rabbit and the Adventure

"I'm bored!" said JJ one day.

"I feel like an adventure."

"An adventure?" asked Mole.

"What's that?"

"It's when you go somewhere new,

and something exciting happens,"

said JJ. "Owl told me."

"I think I feel like an adventure too,"
said Mole.

"Let's go together!" said JJ,
and scampered off into the wood.
"Wait for me!" called Mole.

They bumped into Squirrel.
"Where are you two going
in such a hurry?" he asked.
"We're looking for an adventure,"
said Mole.
"Looking for a what?"
asked Squirrel.

"An adventure," said JJ.
"It's when you go somewhere new
and something exciting happens."
"Can I come too?" said Squirrel.
"Only if you don't run too fast,"
said Mole.

The animals followed a path
which twisted and turned
through the wood.

"Are we there yet?" panted Mole.

"Not yet," said JJ.

"How will we know when we are?"
said Mole.

"When we are somewhere new,"
said Squirrel.

"When something exciting happens,"
said JJ.

The animals walked until they
reached the end of the wood.

But they didn't find an adventure.

Then they walked past a field of corn,

and through a field of turnips.

But nothing exciting happened.

They walked for miles and miles.

They walked past a field of cows,

and over a little bridge.

"I'm tired of looking for an adventure,"

said Squirrel.

"I didn't think adventures were such a long way," said Mole. "Can we stop for a rest now, JJ?" asked Squirrel. "JJ . . .?"

Squirrel looked back along the path.

JJ had disappeared!

Mole and Squirrel
looked behind trees . . .

and under bushes . . .

but there was no JJ.

Suddenly, Squirrel stood still.

"Listen!" he said. "What's that?"

"What's what?" said Mole.

"Ssshh!" whispered Squirrel.

A small voice was calling,

"Help! Help me!"

Mole and Squirrel followed the voice

back along the path to the bridge.

"Help!" it called again.

The voice was getting louder.

"It's JJ!" cried Squirrel.

Mole and Squirrel looked

down over the bridge.

There was poor JJ,

stuck fast in the mud.

"Help!" he squealed.

"I can't move!"

"It's all right," cried Mole.

"We'll save you!"

Squirrel found a long, strong stick
and held it out to JJ.

JJ grabbed the stick with his paws
and held on tight.

Mole and Squirrel held the other end
and pulled.

And pulled . . .

and pulled . . .

At last there was a loud

SQUELCH!

and an even louder

PLOP!

and JJ was free.

"Poor JJ!" said Mole. "What happened?"

"I just came to get a drink." JJ shivered.

"I didn't know the mud would be so

SQUELCHY."

The sun was sinking

lower and lower in the sky.

It was starting to get dark.

"I don't want to look for

adventures any more," said JJ.

"I want to go home."

"I don't think there *are* any

adventures out here," said Mole.

"Which way is home?" asked JJ.

"Over the bridge, past a field of corn

and through a field of cows,"

said Squirrel.

"Or was it over the bridge,

past a field of cows

and then through a field of turnips?"

said Mole, slowly.

"You mean you don't know?" said JJ.

"You mean we're *lost*?"

Mole shivered.

"I don't like being lost," she said.

"Especially not in the dark,"

said Squirrel.

"I want to go home!" wailed JJ.

It was getting darker and darker.

Suddenly they heard

a strange rustling noise.

"What's that?" whispered Squirrel.

"It's a wolf!" cried Mole.

There was more rustling,

followed by a swooshing noise.

"Help!" squealed JJ.

There was another swoosh,
and Owl swooped down from the sky.
"Oh, Owl!" said JJ. "We thought you
were a wolf! We're lost."
"Squirrel doesn't know the way
home," said Mole.
"Nor does Mole!" said Squirrel.
"Oh dear, oh dear," chuckled Owl.
"It's lucky I flew by!"

Three very tired and bedraggled
animals followed Owl as
he led the way.

Soon they were nearly home.

"Look, there's Badger!" said Mole.

Badger was snuffling about,

looking for slugs.

"Where have you all been?" he said.

"We were looking for an adventure,"

said JJ.

44

"But we couldn't find one," said Mole.

"We walked for miles," said JJ,

"then I got stuck in the mud!"

"Then we got lost," said Squirrel,

"and Mole thought there was a wolf."

"But Owl came and saved us!"

cried Mole, happily.

"So you see," said Squirrel,

"there wasn't time for an adventure."

"No," said JJ, with a big yawn,

"but if we get up early tomorrow,

then we might find a *real* adventure."

About the Author and Illustrator

Nicola Moon used to be a science teacher, but now she writes books full-time. She says, "I hope readers will make friends with JJ and his gang, and enjoy sharing their adventures." Nicola Moon's other books for Kingfisher include the I Am Reading title, *Alligator Tails and Crocodile Cakes*.

Ant Parker has illustrated lots of books for children. He doesn't know any rabbits, but he does know a monster who leaves big muddy pawprints all over the house – his dog, Bramble. And Bramble looks just like Badger, too! Ant Parker's other books for Kingfisher include *Flashing Fire Engines* and *Roaring Rockets*.

If you've enjoyed reading *JJ Rabbit and the Monster,*
try these other **I Am Reading** books:

ALLIGATOR TAILS AND CROCODILE CAKES
Nicola Moon & Andy Ellis

BARN PARTY
Claire O'Brien & Tim Archbold

GRANDAD'S DINOSAUR
Brough Girling & Stephen Dell

KIT'S CASTLE
Chris Powling & Anthony Lewis

MISS WIRE AND THE THREE KIND MICE
Ian Whybrow & Emma Chichester Clark

MR COOL
Jacqueline Wilson & Stephen Lewis

MRS HIPPO'S PIZZA PARLOUR
Vivian French & Clive Scruton

PRINCESS ROSA'S WINTER
Judy Hindley & Margaret Chamberlain

WATCH OUT, WILLIAM
Kady MacDonald Denton